D1104445

FOLK TALES FROM THE SOVIET UNION

Compiled by **R. Babloyan** and **M. Shumskaya**
Designed by **M. Anikst**

FOLK TALES FROM THE SOVIET UNION

THE UKRAINE, BYELORUSSIA AND MOLDAVIA

RADUGA PUBLISHERS
MOSCOW

CONTENTS

English translation © Raduga Publishers 1986. Illustrated

ISBN 5-05-001559-6
ISBN 5-05-001561-8

UKRAINIAN FOLK TALES

The Flying Ship
Retold by *Alexander Nechayev*

The Poor Man and the Tsar of the Crows
Retold by *Lidia Kon*
Translations by *Irina Zheleznova*
Illustrated by *Lyudmila Loboda*
and *Ivan Ostafiichuk*

THE FLYING SHIP

There once lived an old man and an old woman who had three sons, two of them clever young men and the third, a fool. The two old people loved their two clever sons dearly, and not a week passed but the old woman would give them each a fresh shirt to wear. But as for the fool, everyone was always mocking and scolding him. He would sit on the stove in his rough linen shirt and if the old woman gave him nothing to eat, hungry he would stay.

One day the news reached the village that the tsar was to hold a feast to which all of his subjects were invited and that the princess would marry him among them who built a flying ship and came flying to the palace in it.

The two clever brothers went to the forest, cut down a tree and began to think how they could build a flying ship out of it when an old man, one as old as old can be, came up to them.

"More power to your elbow!" said he. "And do give me a light, for I want to smoke my pipe."

"We have no time to bother with you, old man!" the brothers replied and began thinking what they were to do about the ship again.

"You'll have a fine trough there for the pigs to eat out of," said the old man, "but you'll no more see the princess than you can see your own ears."

With that he vanished, and as for the two brothers, they tried hard to build the ship and tried again but nothing came of it.

"Let us mount our horses and go to town," said the elder of the two. "We might not marry the princess, but we'll at least take part in the feast."

And the two old people blessed them and helped them to get ready for the journey, the old woman baking them some fine white bread, roasting a whole suckling pig for them and giving them a flask of good Ukrainian vodka to take along with them.

The two brothers mounted their horses and set off on their way, and when the fool learnt about it he began begging his parents to let him follow them.

"I want to go where my brothers went!" said he.

"Do you, you fool!" his mother said. "Why, the wolves will eat you up in the forest."

"No, they won't!"

And there was no doing anything about it, for go he would.

So the old woman got out some stale black bread and filled a flask with water, packed them in a bag, gave the bag to him and sent him on his way.

The fool set off for the forest, and it was when he was nearing it that he saw, coming toward him, an old man, who was as old as old can be and had a snow-white beard that reached to his waist.

"Greetings, Grandpa!" the fool said.

"Greetings to you, my son!"

"Where are you going, Grandpa?"

"I walk all over the earth helping people who are in trouble. And where are you off to?"

"To the tsar's palace where a feast is being held."

"Can you make a ship that can fly of itself, then?"

"No, I can't."

"Then why do you go there?"

"My brothers did, so why shouldn't I! I might make my fortune there."

"Oh, very well. Sit down and let's have a rest and something to eat. Show me what you have in that bag of yours."

"But, Grandpa, all I have there is some stale black bread, you won't like it."

"Never you mind, just take it out."

The fool reached into the bag and brought out some bread, and lo!—it wasn't stale or black at all but very light and fresh and made of the finest wheat, the kind of bread the lords eat on holidays. The fool wondered at the sight of it, but the old man only laughed.

They had a good rest and ate their fill, and the old man thanked the fool and said:

"Listen to me, my son, and do as I say. Go to the forest and find the biggest of the oak-trees there, one whose branches grow crosswise. Strike it three times with your axe and yourself drop to the ground and don't get up till you hear someone calling you. By that time the flying ship will have been built for you, and you can get into it and go wherever you have a mind to. But there is one thing you must do and that is to take along with you whoever it is you meet on your way."

The fool thanked the old man and bade him goodbye. He then went into the forest, found the oak-tree whose branches grew crosswise, struck it three times with his axe, dropped to the ground and fell asleep. By and by he heard someone calling him.

"Get up, for great good fortune has come to you!" the voice said.

The fool jumped up, and lo!—what did he see before him but a flying ship that was made of gold and had masts of silver and sails of silk. All he had to do was to climb into it and go wherever it was he had a mind to.

So in he climbed without another thought, hoisted the sails and was off and away!

And, oh, how fast went the ship and how smoothly!

On and on flew the fool, and when some time had passed, there below him, stretched out on the ground and with one of his ears pressed close to it, he saw a man.

"Good day to you, my good man, and what are you doing there?" the fool called.

"I am listening hard, for I want to hear if the tsar's guests have all gathered at the palace."

"Is that where you are going?"

"Yes!"

"Climb in, then, and I'll take you there."

The man climbed into the ship and away they flew together!

Some time passed, and there below them they saw a man. He was hopping along on one leg and had his other leg tied to his ear.

"Good day to you, my good man!' " the fool called. "Why are you hopping along there on only one leg?"

"If I were to use both legs one step of mine would take me all the way round the earth, and I don't want that!" the man called back.

"Where are you going, then?"

"To the palace, to attend the tsar's feast."

"Climb in with us, and I'll take you there."

"Very well!"

The man climbed into the ship, and away the three of them flew!

Some time passed, and there beneath them they saw an archer taking aim with his bow and arrow. What he was aiming at they could not tell, for round him there spread a wide field with not a bird or a beast in sight.

"Good day to you, my good man!" the fool called. "What are you aiming at? There's not a bird or a beast to be seen anywhere."

"That's what you think! You don't see them, but I do."

"You do?"

"Yes! There's an eagle sitting in an oak-tree beyond that forest there, a hundred miles away from here."

"Come, then, climb in with us!"

The man climbed into the ship and away the four of them flew!

Some time passed, and they saw an old man walking along the road below. He was carrying a sack of bread.

"Where are you going in such haste, Grandpa?" the fool called.

"To get some bread, it'll be dinner-time soon!" the man called back.

"But you have a whole sackful with you!"

"True, but it's not enough for me. One bite, and I'll swallow it all!"

"Come, then, climb in with us!"

The old man climbed into the ship and away the five of them flew!

Some time passed and they saw another old man below them. He was walking along the shore of a lake and seemed to be searching for something.

"What are you doing there, Grandpa?" the fool called.

"Looking for some water, for I'm very thirsty!" the old man called back.

"But there's a lake just in front of you!"

"True, but I can drink all the water in it at one gulp."

"Come then, climb in with us!"

The old man climbed into the ship and away the six of them flew!

Some time passed, and they saw a third old man below them. He had a sack of straw over his shoulder and was trudging along the road.

"Good day to you, Grandpa! Where are you taking the straw?" the fool called.

"To the village yonder."

"Isn't there any straw there?"

"There is, but not the kind I have!"

"And what kind is that?"

"A special kind. No matter how hot the day and how strong the sun, all I have to do is scatter it over the ground and it'll turn to snow."

"Come, then, climb in with us and we'll go to see the tsar together!"

"Very well."

The old man climbed into the ship and away the seven of them flew!

Whether they flew for a long or a short time nobody knows, but they got to the palace and were just in time for the feast.

Kegs of ale and beer had been rolled out into the courtyard, and set up in front of the palace were tables groaning with food: oxen just off the spit, sausages and hams, roasted fowl, gruel and milk, and other good things as well. The kegs stood open, and you could eat and drink your fill!

Present at the feast was half the tsardom: lords and peasants, rich and poor, young and old! And the fool's two clever brothers were there too, sitting side by side at one of the tables.

The fool and his friends came flying up in their golden

ship, they landed just under the tsar's windows, and climbing out of the ship, joined the feasters.

The tsar was much surprised, for never did he think to see a simple peasant step out of the ship! The man was barefoot and had on a pair of pants made of some rough cloth and a shirt with patches all over it.

The tsar clutched his head in horror.

"Never will I let a daughter of mine marry a peasant!" said he to himself.

He began to think how to get rid of the fool and at last decided to give him a number of tasks to do.

"Go and tell that man there," said he to one of his servants, "that he'll not get my daughter in marriage unless he brings me some living water before this feast is over. And if he fails to do it, it'll be out with my sword and off with his head!"

Off went the servant to do the tsar's bidding, but Big-Ear, who heard what the tsar said, passed it all on to the fool.

The fool felt sad and crestfallen. He sat there on the bench with hanging head and could not eat or drink.

"Why so sad?" Fleet-Foot asked him.

"The tsar wants me to bring him some living water before this feast is over, and how am I to do it!"

"Do not grieve, I'll get it for you."

"Well, see that you do!"

The tsar's servant now came up to him and told him what the tsar's orders were, but the fool never turned a hair.

"Tell His Majesty that I will get the living water for him," said he.

He looked at Fleet-Foot who at once untied his leg, the one that was bound to his ear, and was off like a shot! But when he had filled a flask with some living water, which only took him a moment to do, he felt very tired.

"The feast is still in full swing, so I think I'll sit down under this bush here and rest for a bit," said he to himself. And with these words he dropped down on the grass and fell fast asleep. The feast was all but over, and seeing that he had not come back, the fool sat there more dead than alive.

"This is the end of me!" said he to himself.

Big-Ear put his ear to the ground.

"Fleet-Foot is a good-for-nothing if I do say so myself," said he. "He is lying under a bush, fast asleep."

"How'll we wake him?" the fool asked.

The Archer got to his feet.

"I'll do it!" he said.

He drew his bow and shot an arrow straight at the bush, and the branches swayed and scratched Fleet-Foot who jumped up, took one step, and was back at the palace with

18

the living water before the guests had finished eating.

The tsar was much surprised but said nothing. He turned to his servant and bade him tell the fool that he could marry the princess if he and his friends ate up two dozen roasted oxen and a dozen ovenfuls of bread at one swallow. "If they fail to do this," said he, "it'll be out with my sword and off with the fool's head!"

Big-Ear heard this and passed it all on to the fool.

"What am I to do!" the fool cried. "Even one loaf is too much for me to swallow!" And he hung his head and was very sad and crestfallen.

"Don't you grieve, my friend," said Eat-All. "I'll eat it all up by myself and ask for more."

The tsar's servant now came up to the fool and was about to give him the tsar's message, but the fool stopped him, saying:

"I know what the tsar wants me to do. Go and tell the cooks to prepare the food."

The two dozen oxen were soon roasted and a dozen ovenfuls of bread baked, and Eat-All set to with great gusto, polished off all of the food and asked for more.

"I could have done with twice that much!" said he.

Now, this made the tsar very angry, and he ordered the fool and his friends to drink a dozen kegs of beer and a dozen of wine at one gulp.

"If this is not done, it'll be out with my sword and off with the fool's head!" said he.

Big-Ear heard him and passed it all on to the fool again. This time it was Drink-All who came to the fool's aid.

"Never fear, my friend, I'll drink it all up and ask for more," said he.

The tsar's servants rolled out a dozen kegs of beer and a dozen of wine, and Drink-All drained them all at one gulp and left not a drop.

"A meagre treat that!" said he. "I could have drunk twice as much."

The tsar saw that it was not easy to get the better of the fool.

He bade his iron bath-house to be heated till it was red-hot and then ordered the fool to bathe in it.

The fool made for the bath-house together with Freeze-All. They came up to it, and it was as though it was on fire, for the heat fairly took their breath away! But Freeze-All scattered the straw he had with him over the bath-house floor, and it became so cold there that it was all the fool could do to bathe himself at all. He climbed up on to the stove and sat there, trying to warm himself.

And the tsar, thinking that the fool had been burnt to death, sent his servants to the bath-house to see what was left of him.

The servants came inside, and lo!—there was the fool sitting on the stove.

"A poor bath-house this!" said he. "So cold is it here that it's as if it hadn't been heated all winter."

The tsar was quite taken aback, for what was he to do with the fool now!

He thought long and he thought hard and at last he thought of a way of doing away with him.

"The king of the neighbouring land is marching his armies against us," said he, "and not only will I fight him but will test my daughter's suitors at the same time. She shall marry the bravest of the brave among them!"

Many knights now gathered together and went off to fight, and the fool's two elder brothers mounted their horses and joined them, but the fool had no horse and could not do this. He begged the tsar's groom for one, and the groom gave him a dock-tailed nag that could hardly drag itself along the road so very old was it. All the knights had gone on ahead and left him behind them, and there he was unable to get the nag to so much as move from the spot!

All of a sudden whom should he see coming out of the forest and toward him but the old man who had helped him to get the flying ship.

"Do not grieve, my son, I will help you," said he. "As

you will be riding through a large forest you will see a great, spreading lime-tree to the right of you. Tell the lime-tree to open, it will do so, and a saddled horse with a bag tied to the saddle will run out of it. After that if ever you are in need of help just say 'Come, now, out of the bag!' and you'll see what you shall see. And now goodbye."

The fool was overjoyed. He climbed down from his nag's back and ran to the forest where he soon found the great, spreading lime-tree.

"Open, lime-tree!" he cried.

The lime-tree did as he asked, and a most wonderful steed with a mane of gold and a harness so well furbished that it blazed like fire ran out of it. Tied to the saddle was a bag and across it hung a coat of mail, a helmet, a sword and a shield.

The fool put on the helmet and the coat of mail.

"Come, now, out of the bag with you!" he called.

And lo and behold!—huge numbers of men, a whole army, came pouring out of it.

The fool jumped on the steed's back, and riding at a gallop at the army's head, made straight for the enemy. And so well did he fight, hacking away right and left with his sword, that he vanquished one and all. However, towards the battle's end he was wounded in the leg, and it was then that the tsar

and his daughter came riding up on horseback toward him.

Seeing that the knight who had been fighting so bravely was wounded, the princess brought out her kerchief, tore it in two, and bandaged his wound with it.

The fighting over, the fool rode away into the forest and only stopped when he saw the great, spreading lime-tree before him.

"Open, lime-tree!" he cried.

The lime-tree did as he asked, and he hid his horse, his bag, his coat of mail, helmet, sword and shield inside it and put on his patched shirt and worn pants again.

As for the tsar, he now sent his servants to all the corners of the land bidding them find the brave knight whose wound the princess had bandaged with her own kerchief. The servants searched for him among the rich, but could not find him, so the tsar ordered them to search for him among the poor as well. From house to house went the servants, and it was when they had almost given up the search that they came to the fool's hut. It was a poor little place standing at the very edge of the town, and when two of the servants came inside they found the fool's two elder brothers there having their dinner and the fool baking flat-cakes for them. One of his legs was bandaged with the princess's kerchief, and seeing this, the tsar's servants wanted to take him away with them,

but the fool begged them not to, saying that he was much too dirty and unkempt to be shown into the tsar's presence.

"Let me at least go to the bath-house and bathe first," he said. "And you wait for me here and have some dinner."

"Oh, very well, only don't take too long!" said they.

They sat down at the table and began eating the flat-cakes, and the fool ran to the forest and up to the great, spreading lime-tree.

"Open, lime-tree!" he cried.

The lime-tree did as he asked, and the fool's horse ran out of it and waited for the fool to mount him.

The fool now took out the chain-mail and helmet and put them on, and so handsome did he look that none could compare with him. He jumped on the horse's back and rode to the palace, and when the tsar and the princess saw him they were as glad as glad can be! They showered many honours upon him, and he and the princess were married then and there.

THE POOR MAN AND THE TSAR
OF THE CROWS

Once upon a time there lived a poor man who had nothing to his name save a tiny little hut, a strip of land and two small, shaggy bullocks.

And he also had a wife and a whole brood of children who wailed and cried and begged for something to eat from morn to night.

One day the poor man went to the field and he took his youngest son with him. Once there, he began to plough, and he had only finished ploughing two furrows when all of a sudden the sky above him grew very dark just as if night had set in.

He looked up to see if it was a cloud that had hidden the sky from him, and lo!—it was not a cloud but a bird of a kind he had never seen before. Its beak was as sharp as the sharpest of pikes, its claws were as crooked as hooks, and each of its wings was as large as the roof of a house.

The poor man was frightened, as well he might be, for

the bird lighted on the ground and covered him, his son, the two bullocks and the plough with its wings. But he was more frightened still when it spoke to him, saying in a human voice:

"Tell me, my good man, whom shall I take from you, your son or your bullocks? My children are hungry and I must feed them."

"Take neither, take me instead!" the poor man said. "I am old and have had enough of this poor life of mine."

"No," said the bird, "I don't want you. You have smoked far too much in your time, and your flesh is fairly cured by it and might make my children ill if they eat of it. Give me either your son or your bullocks!"

The poor man turned the bird's words over in his mind. What was he to do? He had many children and if he gave up his son to the bird he would still have many left. On the other hand, he had only two bullocks and with them gone he could not hope to finish ploughing his field, bring firewood from the forest or earn any money.

"Don't take so long thinking it over," said the bird. "Tell me who I am to have, your son or your bullocks."

It scratched at the ground with its claws, and seeing how large they were, the poor man felt sorry for his son.

"Come what may, I shall not give up my child!" he told

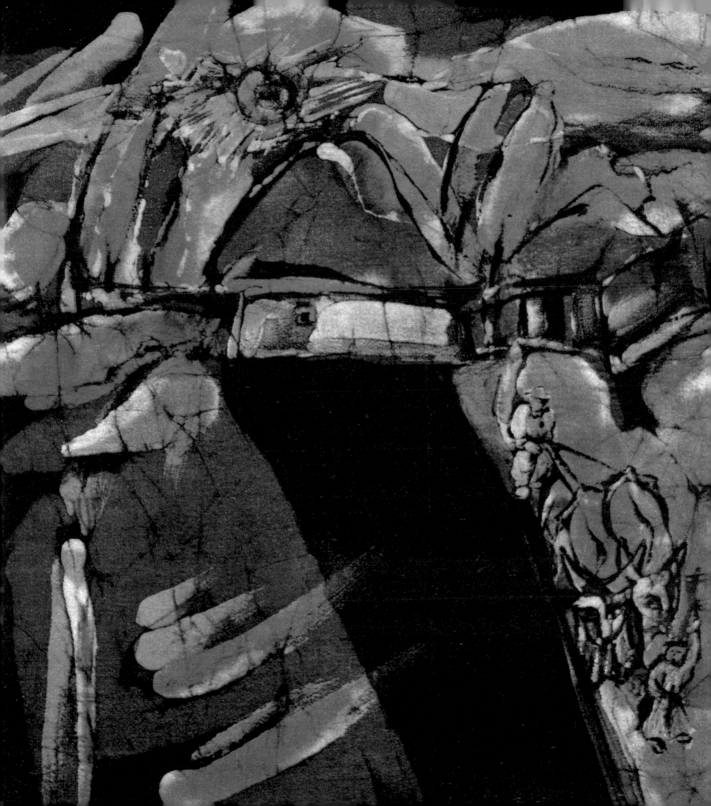

himself, and turning to the bird, said that it could have the bullocks.

"It's lucky for you that you are giving me the bullocks and not your son," said the bird, "for had it been the other way round I would have done you to death together with them. And know this: I will pay you well for the bullocks. Have one of your sons come to my palace, and I will give him whatever he desires."

"Where is your palace to be found?" the poor man asked.

"In a silver glade that lies beyond the steep hills and the dense forests," the bird replied. "Your son must ask of those he meets on the way where the Tsar of the Crows lives, and he will find it."

And with these words it snatched up the two bullocks together with the plough and flew away.

The poor man came back home as sad as sad can be.

"Where are the bullocks?" his wife asked.

He told her of all that had happened and she burst into tears.

"What is to become of us!" she cried. "You haven't ploughed the field or sown it either, so we won't even have any bread."

"Do not cry, Mother," their eldest son said. "I will go to see the Tsar of the Crows and make him pay me for the bullocks. And if I don't come back, my share of the food will be left to the others."

At this the mother began weeping even more bitterly than before.

"Don't go anywhere, son," she said, "we'll find something in the house for you to eat. Why, this terrible bird might eat you up!"

But the boy would not listen to her.

The mother baked him a flat-cake, put the flat-cake and an onion in a bag, gave the bag to him, and bidding him goodbye, sent him on his way.

Off went the eldest son to seek the silver glade where stood the palace of the Tsar of the Crows. He climbed one steep hill and then another, and having crossed two mountain meadows, found himself in a dense forest. Feeling hungry, he seated himself under a bush and took the flat-cake and the onion out of the bag. He had only taken his first bite when there before him, hopping on one leg, he saw a lame crow.

"Greetings, my lad!" the crow said.

"Greetings to you, Crow!" said the elder son.

The crow hopped up a little closer to him.

"I'm very hungry. Won't you give me a piece of your flat-cake?" it said.

"No, I can't do that, find something to eat for your own self," the eldest son replied. "I'm hungry too, and I have a long way to go."

"Where are you going?" the crow asked.

"I am looking for the silver glade where stands the palace of the Tsar of the Crows."

"I am going there too, only my wings and legs are too weak to carry me any further. Let me perch on your shoulder, and I'll show you the way."

"How can I carry you when I can hardly move myself!" the eldest son replied.

At this the crow gave a little hop, flapped its wings and flew away.

This made the eldest son very angry.

"Now, isn't that crow sly!" said he to himself. "It pretended it was lame just so I would carry it."

He put what was left of the flat-cake in his bag and set off again to seek the silver glade where stood the palace of the Tsar of the Crows.

But neither the silver glade nor the palace could he find. He strayed off the path and lost his way in the forest.

The poor man and his wife waited a long time for him to come back, but all in vain. Day followed night and night followed day and there was not a sight or a sign of him.

Said the middle son:

"Bake me a flat-cake, Mother, put the flat-cake and an onion in a bag, give me the bag and a staff, and I'll go in search of my brother. Perhaps I will find the silver glade and the palace of the Tsar of the Crows, and if I do, I'll make the Tsar pay me for the bullocks."

"Don't go anywhere, son," the mother begged. "We'll get on well enough without the Tsar's money. As for your brother, he'll come back without your help if only fate so wills."

But the middle son would not listen to her, and she packed his bag for him and saw him off on his way.

The middle son crossed many green meadows and many dense forests, and one day, as he was walking along, he saw some crows wheeling in the air above him.

"The palace of the Tsar of the Crows must be near here somewhere," said he to himself.

Now, he was in a forest then, a dense one, and feeling hungry, he seated himself under a bush, took the flat-cake and the onion out of his bag and began to eat. All of a sudden a lame old crow appeared before him and began begging him to give it a piece of his flat-cake.

"Your Tsar took away our bullocks, so let him feed you!" the middle son said.

"Well, then, let me at least perch on your shoulder so

33

that hungry and lame as I am I might not die in the forest," said the crow.

"You can perch on your Tsar's shoulder and let him carry you!" the middle son said.

At this the crow gave a little hop, flapped its wings and flew away.

The middle son looked after it in surprise, and getting to his feet, set out on his way again. But neither the silver glade nor the palace of the Tsar of the Crows did he find. For he strayed off the path and lost his way in the forest.

The poor man and his wife waited for their two sons for a long time, but there was not a sight or a sign of them.

Said the youngest son to his mother:

"Please, Mother, pack me a bag of food. Perhaps I will find my brothers and get the Tsar of the Crows to pay us for the bullocks."

The mother burst out crying. She tried to make her son think better of what he meant to do, but all in vain, and in the end she had to let him go.

On and on walked the youngest son and he passed over many green hills and crossed many dense forests. Then, feeling hungry, he seated himself under a bush, the very one under which his two brothers had sat, and began to eat.

He had only just taken his first bite of the flat-cake when

a lame crow appeared before him.

"Do give me a piece of your flat-cake!" it begged, hopping about on one leg.

The youngest son at once broke off a large piece and gave it to the crow.

"Here, eat your fill, you poor thing!" said he. "There's enough here for both of us. And it's a bore to eat by oneself anyway."

"Can I have some of your onion too?" the crow asked.

"Of course you can! I'll be only too glad to share it with you."

The crow ate up the piece of flat-cake and one of the onion and thanked the boy.

"Where is it you are going?" it asked. "Do you know that no one ever found his way out of this forest?"

"I must find the palace of the Tsar of the Crows," said the youngest son. "My brothers must be there."

"Let me perch on your shoulder, for I am lame and my wings are weak," the crow said.

"Why not! I never carried a crow on my shoulder before!" laughed the boy, and he put the crow on his shoulder.

On and on he walked, and the crow pointed out the way for him.

"Turn right! Now turn left! And now go straight ahead!" it told him.

They were on their way for two days and two nights, and they crossed one dense forest and then another. All of a sudden something bright showed ahead and they found themselves in a wide glade. And oh, what a wonderful glade it was, for everything in it, the grass, the flowers and even the stones were of silver.

In the middle of the glade rose a high silver cliff and on the cliff's very top, a palace.

The youngest son stopped and stood there looking at it like one in a trance, for never, not even in his dreams, had he seen anything so beautiful!

He and the crow seated themselves on the edge of the glade and ate up all that remained of the food in the bag.

"That palace you see there is the palace of the Tsar of the Crows," the crow said, "and I'm sure you can find your way to it alone. But you were very kind to me and to repay you for it I will give you a piece of advice. When the Tsar asks you what it is you want him to give you in return for the bullocks, tell him that you want nothing save that which he puts under his pillow before he goes to bed at night."

And with these words the crow vanished.

The youngest son climbed up on to the cliff top, and the palace guards stopped him and led him straight to the silver throne on which sat the Tsar of the Crows.

"How did you find your way here?" the Tsar asked.

The youngest son did not want to let down the crow. "Some kind people showed it me," he said.

"Well, since you have found your way here I must keep my word. Look over my palace, and you shall have whatever it is you like best of all you see in it."

The youngest son walked over the palace for three days and three nights, but he had hardly seen a tenth of it when he decided that it was time to go back to see the Tsar again.

"Yours is a most beautiful palace, Your Majesty," said he to him, "and there is much in it that I liked. But what would I do with such riches? I don't want them. Just give me that which you put under your pillow before you go to bed at night."

The Tsar of the Crows flew into a rage.

"How did the lad get to learn about it?" he cried. "One of the crows must have told him about it!" And he gave orders for all the crows who had been showing the youngest son around the palace to have their heads cut off. Then, turning to the youngest son, he began trying to get him to change his mind about what it was he had asked for.

"Do not ask me for that which you cannot have," he said. "I will give you many bullocks and a wagonload of gold if you like."

"No, I want nothing save that which you put under your

pillow before you go to bed at night!" said the youngest son.

"That you cannot have. Take everything I have in this palace instead!" the Tsar said.

But the youngest son stood his ground, and there was nothing the Tsar could do.

He took a little coffee-grinder from under his pillow, and giving it to the boy, cried:

"Here, take it, only get out of my sight before I have you pecked to death!"

The youngest son put his grinder in his bag and ran out of the palace, and he only stopped when he found himself in the forest again.

He sat down for a rest, brought out the grinder and reached into the bag again to see if there was a piece of the flat-cake left there. But the bag was empty, and the boy told himself that it was a poor counsel the lame crow had given him.

"What do I need this grinder for!" thought he. "I should have asked for some gold or for some food even. This way I'll starve to death and never get back home at all."

But then, remembering that the Tsar of the Crows had been willing to give up all his riches to him if only he left him the coffee-grinder he began looking it over. It seemed a simple enough thing and had a handle on one side of it like any coffee-grinder.

"I wish I had a table before me laden with food and drink, like the one the Tsar of the Crows had in his palace!" said he to himself, and without thinking about it, gave the handle a twist.

The same moment a table covered with a rich cloth and groaning with food and drink appeared before him.

The boy was overjoyed.

"Just see what this grinder can do!" he cried.

But he felt sad again the next moment, saying to himself:

"This won't do at all! Here I am sitting at this table and eating and drinking all by myself while my mother and father and my bothers and sisters go hungry."

And turning the handle again, he said aloud:

"Let my mother and father and all my brothers and sisters appear before me!"

And no sooner were the words out of his mouth than his whole family, mother, father, sisters and brothers, were there before him. They began eating and drinking and they never stopped till they had polished off everything!

After that they all went back home together and lived together very happily ever after, for the grinder gave them everything they needed.

Now, if you don't believe me, pay them a visit, and they'll tell you all about it if they want to.

THE BYELORUSSIAN FOLK TALE

Teeny-Tiny

Retold by *Alexander Yakimovich*

Translated by *Irina Zheleznova*

Illustrations by *Vladimir Savich*

TEENY-TINY

There once lived an old man and an old woman who had no children. One day the old man dreamt that someone told him to go to the forest, gather some birds' eggs there and hatch babies out of them.

The old man told the old woman about it.

"Why don't you do it, then, old man!" the old woman said. "Go to the forest and gather some eggs, and then we'll put the eggs in a sieve and I'll sit on them till they are hatched. The baby birds will start to chirp and to twitter and we'll think them to be our children and feel the happier for it."

The old man did as his wife said. He went to the forest and climbed a birch-tree, but when he looked in the nest that he found there he saw that there was only one egg in it. He climbed a second birch-tree and found a second nest, but in it too there was only one egg. All in all he climbed thirty birches and found one egg in each of the nests save the last which held two. He now had thirty-one eggs and told himself that that was enough. He brought the eggs home and put them in a sieve, and the old woman sat down on them just as though she were a hen.

Three weeks or so went by, and not baby birds but baby boys were hatched out of them.

"Look, old man, you and I have sons, thirty-one of them!" the old woman said.

The old man was overjoyed. He invited two of his friends and their wives over to his house, and, setting a jug of wine on the table before them, harnessed a horse and set out for the priest's house to ask him to baptize his children.

He was soon back, bringing the priest, who baptized all thirty-one of the boys and gave a name to each save the youngest and weakest of them. He told the old man and the old woman that he could think of no name for him and that they could give him any name they chose, and seeing that the boy was so very small, the old man and the old woman named him Teeny-Tiny.

The boys grew very fast, not by the day but by the hour, and they were quite grown up by the time a year had passed.

"Why do we only play games and do nothing else, Father?" asked they. "It's time for us to do some work. Go into town

and buy scythes for us, and we'll cut the grass!"

The old man rode off to town and bought thirty scythes, but though he looked all over he could not find a scythe small enough for Teeny-Tiny to handle. He rode home and he called his sons.

"Here, my sons, choose a scythe for yourself, each of you!" said he.

The sons each chose a scythe for himself, but when Teeny-Tiny came up to his father there was none for him:

"Where's my scythe, Father?" he asked.

"I couldn't find one for you, my son," the father said. "I'm old and you're very young, so the two of us will stay at home and not do any work."

"Oh, well, let it be as father bids," the thirty elder brothers said, and off they went to cut the grass.

They came to their father's meadow, which lay three miles or so away from their house, and finding it to be quite large, divided it up into plots in such a way that each of them now had a plot of his own and two were left for their father and for Teeny-Tiny.

Some time passed, and Teeny-Tiny, who had stayed at home with his father, said to him:

"I think I'll go and see how my brothers are making out with their work, Father."

"Very well, my son, but see that you don't lose your way," the father said.

"I'll try not to."

But no sooner had he left the house than he strayed off the path, found himself in a forest and could not find his way out of it.

He climbed an oak-tree and looked all about him, and he saw his brothers, all thirty of them, wielding their scythes quite close to where he was. He seized the oak-tree by its crown and bent it to the ground, and lo!—it split in two. Then, tearing off the branches, he threw the tree over his shoulder and made straight for the meadow where his brothers were.

"Work away, and may God be with you, my brothers!" he said. "Only why have you left two of the plots untouched? Do they belong to someone else?"

"We left the two plots for you and father to work on," the brothers said.

"But didn't father say I was too young and he was too old to work!"

"If you can't work yourselves you can hire someone else to do the work for you!"

"Oh, very well, then!" said Teeny-Tiny.

He took off his hat, and set to work.

He used the oak-tree he had with him to cut the grass and rake it, and he had the two plots, his and his father's, mowed and the stack made before his brothers had finished mowing their plots or made their stacks.

The brothers, Teeny-Tiny among them, came back home together, and their father asked them if the grass was all cut.

"Yes, Father, all of it!" the thirty elder brothers said.

"Not all of it!" said Teeny-Tiny.

"What do you mean?" the father asked.

"Just that my brothers left two of the plots for you and me to mow," said Teeny-Tiny.

"Didn't I say that I was too old to work!" the father said.

"Don't you grieve, Father, for I mowed the two plots myself and made a stack of the hay."

The father turned to his thirty elder sons.

"What about you, did you make only one stack too?" he asked.

"No," said they. "We each of us mowed one plot and we have thirty stacks to show for it."

"You had better watch over them if you don't want the hay to be stolen," the father said.

Evening came, and ten of the brothers went to the meadow to watch over the hay. They stayed there all night long, but when morning came found that one of the stacks was gone.

They came home, and their father asked them if the hay was safe.

"Not all of it," said they. "One of the stacks has been stolen."

The father flew into a temper.

"Fools, all ten of you!" he cried. "How could you let this happen!"

On the second evening ten other of the brothers went to the meadow. They watched over the hay all night, but when morning came found that another of the stacks was gone.

On the third evening the last ten of the brothers went to the meadow. They watched over the hay all night, but when morning came found that yet another of the stacks was gone.

On the fourth evening it was the turn of the first ten brothers to watch over the hay again, but they did not want to do it and told Teeny-Tiny that there was a hay stack of his in the meadow and that he should be the one to keep watch over the hay for a change.

"Very well," said Teeny-Tiny, "I'll do it if I must," and, turning to his father, he added: "Please, Father, go to the blacksmith and ask him to forge me an iron cudgel weighing thirty poods."

The father did as Teeny-Tiny asked, and the blacksmith forged Teeny-Tiny the cudgel.

And Teeny-Tiny seized the cudgel and hurled it up so high that it vanished from sight. Then, seeing it come flying down again, he lifted his head, and the cudgel struck his forehead and broke into four pieces.

Teeny-Tiny called his father.

"Please, Father, have the blacksmith forge me another cudgel, one weighing forty poods," said he.

The blacksmith forged another cudgel, and Teeny-Tiny took it and hurled it up again, but, unlike the first one, it did not vanish from sight. He lifted his head as it came flying down, but when it hit his forehead it did not break and was only dented a little.

"This one will do!" said Teeny-Tiny, and picking up the cudgel, he set out for the meadow to watch over the hay.

He came up to his haystack, climbed to its top and sat there. All of a sudden he heard a clatter so great that it made the earth quake. He sprang to his feet and saw a mare followed by thirty-one colts come running toward him.

They ran up to Teeny-Tiny's haystack, and standing round

it in a circle, began eating the hay. Teeny-Tiny waited till only a little of the hay was left and then he seized the mare by the mane and sprang on her back. Away ran the mare, carrying Teeny-Tiny, who goaded her on with his cudgel, over fields and forests, and it was only when she was quite spent and worn that she stopped at last.

"Do let me go free, Teeny-Tiny," she begged, "and I will give you whatever you ask for."

"I want those colts of yours!" said Teeny-Tiny.

"Take them, then, only set me free!"

"You won't try to trick me, will you?"

"No."

She carried him back to the haystack, and there were the colts still, eating what was left of the hay.

"Get on the back of the biggest of the colts," said the mare. "The other thirty will follow it."

"Even if all thirty of them run away, I'll still have one left, and it will be enough to pay for the hay!" said Teeny-Tiny to himself.

He got on the back of the biggest of the colts and rode away, and the other colts ran after them.

He came back home and rode into the yard, but the yard was small and there wasn't enough room in it for all of the colts.

58

Teeny-Tiny called his brothers.

"Come here, brothers, and each of you choose a colt for yourself!" he cried. "I caught them when I saw them eating up our hay."

Each of the brothers chose a colt for himself, and fine colts they were, but there was only a poor little lame one left, who had come dragging himself along after the rest, for Teeny-Tiny.

"There's my colt!" said Teeny-Tiny, and his brothers stood there laughing at him, for wasn't he a fool to have caught all those colts and been left with the worst of them!

"There's nothing I can do with you, you ninnies!" said Teeny-Tiny. "You have taken the best colts for yourselves, yet you stand there laughing! But never you mind, this one is good enough for me."

The brothers all took good care of their colts, and when the colts had grown they got collars for them and bought some wagons and then set to work ploughing the fields and carrying firewood from the forest.

After a time they built themselves a farmhouse and a yard and had as good a life as anyone could wish for.

But when three or four years had passed, they began to feel bored and restless and decided that it was time to leave home and go travelling. And as to what might happen later, well, that was in fate's hands: some of them might marry, some take up service with someone.

"You must go without me, for I'm staying home, brothers," said Teeny-Tiny. "Mother and father are no longer young, and who will there be to lay them to rest if all of us leave home!"

"Very well, stay home if you wish!" the brothers said. "Only you'll never catch us up if you do!"

"Oh, yes I will!" said Teeny-Tiny.

The brothers set out on their way, and Teeny-Tiny stayed at home.

A year passed, the father died, and Teeny-Tiny put him to rest.

Another year passed, and the mother died, and Teeny-Tiny put her to rest too and held a wake in both his parents' memory. After that he called together the men from his village and asked if there was anyone among them willing to rent his farm. "If I return I'll want it back," said he, "but if I don't, I won't."

Now, the farm was a big farm and richer than those of many of the rich landowners, and none of the peasants wanted it.

So then he spoke to one of the landowners and left his house and lands to him, asking no rent for them and with only a receipt in return and a promise that they would be taken good care of.

As for his colt, what with the care he lavished on it and the good food he gave it, sharing with it whatever it was he ate himself, it had grown into a fine horse, finer by far than those of his brothers. He had even taught it to speak which was a marvel if ever there was one.

The farm off his hands, Teeny-Tiny sold his grain, and taking the money he got for it with him, rode after his brothers.

The brothers had been on their way for three years, but Teeny-Tiny caught them up in only three months.

"Greetings, brothers!" he called.

"Greetings to you, Teeny-Tiny!" the brothers called back. "How are things back home? Are mother and father well?"

"They are both dead, alas, but I hope and trust that you are all well and have had a good journey. Do tell me about it."

"We have had a very good journey indeed," the brothers said. "But why don't you take the lead and ride at the head of us now?"

Teeny-Tiny did as they said, and on they all rode. A whole day passed but there were only forests and fields about them and never a village in sight.

The sun had just set when they came to a forest where,

turning round and round, stood a little hut on chicken feet.

"Please, hut, stop and turn no more, let me enter through the door!" Teeny-Tiny cried.

The hut stopped turning, and Teeny-Tiny went inside. And lo!—whom should he see there but *Baba-Yaga the Leg of Stone, a very, very old and wicked crone. She was stretched on the floor, her head near the door, and so twisted was she that she seemed to be kneeling, for her nose reached the garret and her mouth touched the ceiling!*

"Greetings, Baba-Yaga!" said Teeny-Tiny.

"Greetings to you, Teeny-Tiny! What are you after? Where are you going?"

"I am travelling round the world with my brothers, and what is to be will be. Some of us may marry, some take up service with someone."

"Are there many of you?"

"Thirty-one, all told."

"A pity I have only twenty-nine daughters and not thirty-one, for then you could have married them. But never mind! Just ride on farther and go to see my sister."

Teeny-Tiny left the hut and he and his brothers rode on.

They rode and they rode, and some ten hours had passed

when they came to a second hut. It too had chicken feet and was turning round and round.

"Please, hut, stop and turn no more, let me enter through the door!" Teeny-Tiny cried.

The hut stopped turning, Teeny-Tiny went inside, and whom should he see there but *Baba-Yaga the Leg of Stone, a very, very old and wicked crone. She was stretched on the floor, her head near the door, and so twisted was she that she seemed to be kneeling, for her nose reached the garret and her mouth touched the ceiling.*

"Greetings, Baba-Yaga!" said Teeny-Tiny.

"Greetings to you, Teeny-Tiny! What are you after? Where are you going?"

"I am travelling over the world with my brothers, and what is to be will be. Some of us may marry and some take up service with someone."

"Are there many of you?"

"Thirty-one, all told."

"A pity I have only thirty daughters and not thirty-one, for then you could have married them. But never mind! Just ride on farther and go to see my sister."

They rode on and soon came to a third hut. It had chicken feet like the first two and was turning round and round.

"Please, hut, stop and turn no more, let me enter through the door!" Teeny-Tiny cried.

The hut stopped, Teeny-Tiny went inside, and whom should he see there but *Baba-Yaga the Leg of Stone, a very, very old and wicked crone. She was stretched on the floor, her head near the door, and so twisted was she that she seemed to be kneeling, for her nose reached the garret and her mouth touched the ceiling!*

"Greetings, Baba-Yaga!" said Teeny-Tiny.

"Greetings to you, Teeny-Tiny! What are you after? Where are you going?"

"I am travelling over the world with my thirty brothers, and what is to be will be. Some of us may marry and some take up service with someone."

"A good thing you came here! I have thirty-one daughters, and they'll make good brides for you. So ride into the yard and unharness your horses, and I'll have oats and hay given them."

They rode into the yard and unharnessed their horses, and there were the oats and the hay all ready and waiting for them!

They came into the hut, and Baba-Yaga gave them food and drink and then called her daughters who turned out to be very comely maids indeed, each more beautiful than the other.

64

"Well, my lads," said Baba-Yaga, "now each of you must choose the one you like best of my daughters and wish to marry!"

This the brothers did, and Baba-Yaga told them to go to bed.

"We are going to have the wedding tomorrow!" said she.

The brothers did as she said and were soon asleep, all save Teeny-Tiny who went out into the yard to talk to his horse.

"*You think to be wed, but you'll all die instead*, Teeny-Tiny!" said the horse.

"How is that?" Teeny-Tiny asked.

"Baba-Yaga means to kill you," the horse replied. "Listen to me and do as I say. Before going to bed you must exchange your own and your brothers' hats for her daughters' kerchiefs. Let the maids wear the hats and your brothers and you, the kerchiefs. Baba-Yaga has a sword that smites of itself. She will get up at midnight and send it at those of you who will be wearing hats. Do not sleep but watch and see where she keeps the sword, and as soon as it cuts off the maids' heads run away together with your brothers."

Teeny-Tiny did as the horse said. No sooner was everyone asleep than he exchanged the hats for the kerchiefs, and lying down again, waited to see what would happen.

66

By and by Baba-Yaga sniffed and cocked an ear, and thinking that everyone was asleep, took the sword that smote of itself from the stove ledge.

"Cut off the heads that have hats on them, my sword!" said she in a whisper.

The sword cut off her daughters' heads, but not knowing this and telling herself that she would take the heads away in the morning, Baba-Yaga went back to bed again and was soon sound asleep.

Seeing her, Teeny-Tiny woke his brothers and they all crept out of the hut.

"Let's not tarry but be off at once!" said Teeny-Tiny.

"How is that! Aren't we going to get married?" his brothers asked.

"Get married indeed! You can thank your stars that you aren't all dead!" Teeny-Tiny said.

They got on their horses' backs and urged them on, and they were some two hundred miles away from her hut when Baba-Yaga woke. She looked at her daughters and saw that they were all dead.

"You are a sly one, Teeny-Tiny!" she cried. "But you won't get away from me, I will catch you up all the same!"

Now, she had three goats in her stable, so she led out one of them, got on its back and began goading it on with her iron pestle.

She was out to catch up Teeny-Tiny, and lo!—she had caught him up in three hours or so.

"You could not get away from me, could you, Teeny-Tiny!" she cried.

They began to fight, they fought for three hours, and at the end of them Teeny-Tiny killed Baba-Yaga's goat.

"You wait, I'll get my hands on you yet!" Baba-Yaga cried.

"We'll see about that!" said Teeny-Tiny.

Baba-Yaga said no more but turned away and went home on foot, and he and his brothers rode on.

All round the world they travelled, but to turn back and go home seemed silly, so they became soldiers. They told the tsar whose army they joined, who they were and where they had come from and they served him faithfully.

Some time passed, and the tsar promoted Teeny-Tiny to corporal and put him in charge of his brothers.

Now, the brothers did not like this at all, for was not Teeny-Tiny the youngest of them, so they went to the tsar and told him that there was one *Baba-Yaga the Leg of Stone, a very very old and wicked crone,* who lived beyond the thrice-nine lands in the thrice-ten tsardom, that she had a sword that smote of itself and could even gather together the heads

it chopped off and that none save Teeny-Tiny could get the sword for him.

The tsar sent for Teeny-Tiny.

"Is it true that beyond the thrice-nine lands, in the thrice-ten tsardom there lives *Baba-Yaga the Leg of Stone, a very very old and wicked crone* and that she has a sword that smites of itself?" he asked. "If it is, then you must get the sword for me."

"It's true enough that there is such a sword, but to get it is something no one can do," Teeny-Tiny said.

The tsar flew into a temper.

"How dare you refuse to do what I tell you to!" he cried. "Why, I'll have your head cut off this minute!"

"Very well, I'll try to get the sword for you," said Teeny-Tiny. "Only give me three hours to think over how I am to go about it."

He went to the stable and told his horse that he was very unhappy.

"And why would that be?" the horse asked.

"Oh, it's just that the tsar wants me to do something I cannot do," Teeny-Tiny said.

"And what is that?"

"I am to get him the sword that smites of itself."

"That's nothing, there are harder things to come! So

74

say your prayer and go to bed, for night is the mother of wisdom."

Teeny-Tiny did as the horse said. He went to the tsar, told him that he would get the sword for him, said his prayers and went to bed. And on the following morning he rose very early, washed, said his prayers again, got on his horse and set out at a gallop for Baba-Yaga's house.

He was there on the stroke of midnight.

"Do you know where the sword that smites of itself is kept?" the horse asked.

"I do!" said Teeny-Tiny.

"Well, then, go and get it. But don't waste time and mind that Baba-Yaga doesn't hear you, she's asleep now!"

Teeny-Tiny went into the hut, took the sword that smote of itself from its place on the stove ledge, slipped out through the door, and getting on his horse, rode back to the tsar's palace.

It was dawning when Baba-Yaga woke, and she at once felt that someone had been in her house. She looked at the stove ledge, and seeing that the sword was gone, guessed that it was Teeny-Tiny who had taken it. So she got on her goat's back, and goading it on with her iron pestle, rode after Teeny-Tiny.

"You won't get away from me this time!" she cried,

seeing him ahead of her.

She caught him up and went at him, and they began to fight. Long and hard they fought and only stopped when Teeny-Tiny killed Baba-Yaga's goat.

Off went Baba-Yaga home on foot, saying over and over again:

"You wait, Teeny-Tiny, I'll get my hands on you yet! Then we'll see what we shall see!"

Teeny-Tiny brought the sword that smote of itself to the tsar who was so pleased that he promoted him to sergeant.

Teeny-Tiny's brothers were more envious than ever. They went to see the tsar and told him that that same Baba-Yaga the Leg of Stone who lived beyond the thrice-nine lands in the thrice-ten tsardom had a *gusli** that played of itself and that could dance and sing songs as well.

"None save Teeny-Tiny can get that *gusli* for you, Your Majesty," said they.

The tsar sent for Teeny-Tiny.

"Is it true that *Baba-Yaga the Leg of Stone, a very, very old and wicked crone,* has a *gusli* that plays, dances and sings of itself?" he asked.

Gusli—an ancient Russian string instrument.—*Tr.*

"This is the first I hear of it, Your Majesty!" said Teeny-Tiny.

"Go and fetch the *gusli* and don't refuse or I'll have your head cut off!" said the tsar.

It could not be helped, so Teeny-Tiny went to see his horse again and told him that he was very, very unhappy.

"Why would that be?" the horse asked.

"It's just that the tsar wants me to do something I cannot do," Teeny-Tiny said.

"And what is that?"

"I am to get him the *gusli* that belongs to Baba-Yaga the Leg of Stone and that plays, dances and sings of itself, and I never even heard of such a thing."

"Well, there is such a thing, and get it we will!" said the horse. "Just jump on my back and hold tight! We'll be at Baba-Yaga's house in no time at all."

Away they went at a gallop and were soon at the door of Baba-Yaga's house.

Said the horse to Teeny-Tiny:

"Go into the house and you'll see the *gusli* lying on the stove ledge. Be careful how you handle it, for it might start to play and Baba-Yaga will hear it and kill you! She has gone out, but she can't be far."

Teeny-Tiny came into the house, climbed up on the stove

78

ledge, and taking the *gusli* that played of itself, hurried out with it. But when he got on his horse's back, he began to sing, and this made the horse very angry.

"Hush now or Baba-Yaga will kill you!" he said, and away he galloped.

They were some two hundred miles away from her hut when Baba-Yaga saw that her *gusli* was gone. She did not wait but got on her third goat, and waving her iron pestle, goaded it on with it.

She caught up Teeny-Tiny, and they began to fight. They fought for a day and they fought for a night, and Teeny-Tiny killed the goat.

"I'll never forgive you for this, Teeny-Tiny!" Baba-Yaga cried, tears of rage running from her eyes.

And Teeny-Tiny went back to the palace and gave the *gusli* that played of itself to the tsar. The tsar took it and touched the strings, and the *gusli* at once began to play, to dance and to sing. And so loudly did it play and sing that the sound of it carried all over the tsardom.

The tsar was pleased and promoted Teeny-Tiny again, and Teeny-Tiny, who was very angry with his brothers for having twice done him an ill turn, was even more strict with them now than before.

Now, it was then or a little while later that the sun was

seen to stand still and not move from its place in the sky for a full three hours. And Teeny-Tiny's brothers, who thought to profit by this, at once went to see the tsar and told him that none save Teeny-Tiny could find out why this had happened.

The tsar sent for Teeny-Tiny.

"I want you to find out why the sun stood still and did not move from its place in the sky for three whole hours!" said he.

Teeny-Tiny was quite taken aback.

"I can't do that, Your Majesty, no one can!" said he.

"You must all the same or I'll have your head cut off!" the tsar cried.

"Oh, very well, only give me three hours to think over how I am to go about it, Your Majesty," Teeny-Tiny said.

Off he went to see his horse and told him with tears in his eyes that his end had come.

"What makes you say that, Teeny-Tiny?" the horse asked.

"The tsar bids me do something I cannot do!" Teeny-Tiny said.

"And what is that?"

"I am to find out why the sun stood still for three hours."

"That's nothing, there are harder things to come!" said

the horse. "Get on my back and let us be off!"

They rode for a day and a night and for another day and another night, and they came to the seashore. And lo!—there before them, stretched across the sea, was a huge Whale-Fish, a thing of wonder if ever there was one. People were using him for a bridge, and Teeny-Tiny told his horse to do the same.

"Where are you going, Teeny-Tiny?" the Whale-Fish asked.

"I want to see the sun and ask it why it stood still for three hours," said Teeny-Tiny.

"Well, then, you can ask it at the same time why I have been forced to lie on my side, with people walking and riding across me, for three whole years now. Do this for me, and I will help you out too some day."

"Very well, I'll see what I can do!" said Teeny-Tiny.

On he rode across the Whale-Fish and only stopped when he came to the place where the sun was known to set. Before him stood a mud hut, he went inside, and whom should he see there but the half-moon! The sun was out, and the half-moon was waiting for it to come back.

Teeny-Tiny greeted the half-moon who asked him why he had come so far.

"I want to ask the sun why it stood still for three whole hours," Teeny-Tiny explained.

"Well, then, Teeny-Tiny, take this coat, it is lined with fur, as you can see, turn it inside out, put it on and hide behind the stove," the half-moon said. "And mind you do it quickly! For the sun will soon come and it might burn you to death if you don't. Just stay hidden, and I will keep it busy talking until it cools."

Teeny-Tiny did as the half-moon said, and lo!—there was the sun on the doorstep. The whole of the hut was lit up by its rays, and it became so hot that Teeny-Tiny would have been burnt to a cinder if it wasn't for the coat he had on.

"There's someone here come to see you," said the half-moon to the sun. "He wants to know why you stood without moving for three whole hours."

"Where is he?"

"Behind the stove."

"Behind the stove?" said the sun, and shouted: "Climb out, whoever you are, and let me see you!"

Teeny-Tiny climbed out from behind the stove and bowed low to the sun who asked him who he was and where he had come from. Teeny-Tiny told it all it wanted to know, and the sun said:

"There is a maid named Volinka living by the sea. She has a golden boat and a golden paddle, and she paddles the boat herself and steers it too. There is not another maid in the world so beautiful, and it was because I could not take my eyes off her that I stood without moving for three hours."

Teeny-Tiny stared at the sun round-eyed.

"Who could have thought it!" said he. "And now, sun, do tell me why the Whale-Fish has been made to lie on his side for three whole years. How long is he to lie so?"

"Let him spit out the forty ships he swallowed and never swallow another, and he will be free to roam the seas again," the sun said. "Only don't tell him this until you have crossed him, for he might turn over, and you'll be drowned."

Teeny-Tiny bowed low to the sun and rode back to his tsardom and up to the Whale-Fish who asked if he had spoken to the sun about him.

"I'll tell you that when I'm on the other side of the sea," Teeny-Tiny said, and he rode across the Whale-Fish.

"The sun told me that you will only be able to roam the seas in freedom again when you spit out the forty ships and everything else you swallowed!" he shouted.

The Whale-Fish was overjoyed.

"Hurry and ride away!" he cried. "For I am going to turn over and shake myself, and the waves might carry you off to sea."

He did as the sun bade, and having thus atoned for his sins, went roaming the blue seas again.

And Teeny-Tiny went back to the tsar's palace and told the tsar about Volinka, the beautiful maid who sailed the seas in a golden boat and paddled and steered it herself.

"There is none to compare with her," he said. "And it was because the sun could not take its eyes off her that it stood still for three whole hours."

The tsar was pleased with Teeny-Tiny and promoted him yet again.

Whether a long or a short time passed nobody knows but the tsar began thinking about Volinka and about how he was to get a look at her. He ordered Teeny-Tiny to fetch her, and remembering that the Whale-Fish had promised to repay him for what he did for him, Teeny-Tiny said that he would think it over and would perhaps be able to do it.

He went to see his horse, and as he came into the stable, the tears poured from his eyes.

"Why so sad, Teeny-Tiny?" the horse asked.

"How can I help it! The tsar wants me to do something I cannot do again."

"And what is that?"

"He bids me fetch Volinka, *a maid fair beyond compare,*

who sails the seas in a golden boat and paddles and steers it herself."

"That's nothing! Go to the tsar, ask him to give you all sorts of fruits and delicacies from overseas, and we'll set out on our way."

Teeny-Tiny went to see the tsar.

"Please, Your Majesty, do not punish me but let me have my say," said he. "I must have three hundred rubles worth of fruits and delicacies from overseas."

The tsar gave him all he asked for, and Teeny-Tiny took it all and went back to his horse.

"The tsar gave me everything you told me to ask him for," said he.

"Take a tent, and we'll go to the seashore," the horse said.

They came to the seashore, and the horse told Teeny-Tiny to set him free and let him roam the green fields.

"And you must set up a tent and bring out the fruits and delicacies," he said. "And when you see Volinka sailing past, knock one spoon against another. Volinka will hear the sound of it, and she will sail up close to the tent and ask you who you are and when it was you came there. Be nice to her and try to please her, and don't forget to offer her the fruits and other good things."

Teeny-Tiny did as the horse said. He set up his tent on the seashore and brought out all the fruits and delicacies he had with him. After that he seated himself and settled down to wait.

All of a sudden he saw something gleaming on the water and at once knew it to be Volinka's boat. The maid had a golden paddle in her hand and she was plying it and steering the boat to shore. And as she did so she kept glancing at the tent.

"Who are you? When did you come here?" she called, paddling up close. "I have sailed past many a time, but I never saw a tent here before."

"I only came here a little while ago," said Teeny-Tiny. "But do sail up nearer and try some of my fruits. They are very good."

Volinka sailed up nearer and held out her paddle, and Teeny-Tiny put a great, juicy peach on it.

Volinka ate it and began plying her paddle again, but she had not sailed far before she decided that she would like another. She sailed back to shore again, asked Teeny-Tiny for another peach and held out her paddle, and Teeny-Tiny put a peach on it. This she ate, but instead of sailing away, told Teeny-Tiny that she was very thirsty.

"Would you care for some juice?" Teeny-Tiny asked.

"Yes, please!" Volinka said, holding out her paddle.

Teeny-Tiny poured her a cup of grape juice.

"You would make me very happy if you took the cup from my hands," he said.

Volinka paddled up closer still and stretched out her hand for the cup, and Teeny-Tiny seized her hand and held it.

"I've caught you, my fair one!" he cried.

He whistled to his horse, who at once came running up to him, took all he had brought with him, placed the maid in front of him on the horse's back and set out on his way back to the palace.

The tsar met them at the door, and when he saw how beautiful Volinka was, he fell head over ears in love with her.

In his joy he promoted Teeny-Tiny to captain, and was so eager to marry the maid that he could hardly wait.

"Surely you don't think that I can get married in this gown!" the maid said. "My trousseau is in an iron chest which weighs all of three hundred poods and lies at the bottom of the sea. Have the chest brought to me, and I'll dress as becomes a bride!"

It could not be helped, so the tsar sent for Teeny-Tiny and ordered him to fetch the chest.

"But, Your Majesty, it can't be done, no one can do it," said Teeny-Tiny.

"You had better do it, though, or I'll have your head cut off!" the tsar said.

"Give me a little time to think how to go about it, then."

"You can think all you like just so you fetch the chest!"

Teeny-Tiny went to see his horse again.

"You don't know how unhappy I am!" he said.

"And why is that?" the horse asked.

"Because the tsar bids me fetch him an iron chest weighing all of three hundred poods which lies at the bottom of the sea, that's why."

"Oh, is that all!" the horse said. "Just you go to the tsar and ask him for the sword that smites of itself."

Teeny-Tiny did as the horse said. He went to the tsar, got the sword, and coming back again, climbed on the horse's back and rode off at a gallop for the sea.

They were there soon enough, and the horse told him to cast the sword into the sea and let it cut off the heads of the smaller of the fishes.

Teeny-Tiny cast the sword into the sea.

"Cut off the small fishes' heads, sword, and gather them together!" he cried.

The sword set to cutting off the small fishes' heads, and the Whale-Fish saw it and came swimming up to Teeny-Tiny.

"Stop, Teeny-Tiny, spare my kin, and I will do whatever you ask of me!" he cried.

"I want the iron chest that weighs three hundred poods and lies at the bottom of the sea!" said Teeny-Tiny.

The Whale-Fish sent some fish for the chest, and they brought it up from the bottom of the sea and gave it to him.

"And now, Teeny-Tiny," said the Whale-Fish, "make off on your horse and do not stop till you are two hundred miles away from here. I will then throw the chest to you and you must try to catch it. If you don't, it will fall through the ground, and none will ever be able to find it."

Teeny-Tiny took the sword that smote of itself and away he rode!

He made good time and had left two hundred miles between himself and the Whale-Fish when he heard a great clanging and thumping and knew that it was the chest flying through the air toward him. He held out his arms and caught it, and before he knew where he was, found himself in the tsar's palace again.

The tsar promoted him to major and then asked Volinka to marry him again.

"I can't do that, I must unlock the chest first!" Volinka said. "Have them fetch me the golden key that weighs all of five hundred poods and lies at the bottom of the sea!"

The tsar sent for Teeny-Tiny and bade him fetch the key.

This time Teeny-Tiny did not argue. He took the sword that smote of itself and away he rode for the sea! And no sooner was he there than he cast the sword into the sea and told it to cut off the middle fishes' heads.

The sword did as he said, and lo and behold!—there was the Whale-Fish swimming up to him.

"What would you have me do, Teeny-Tiny?" he asked.

"I want you to fetch me the golden key that lies at the bottom of the sea."

"Tell your sword to spare my kin, and you shall have it!" the Whale-Fish said, and he sent some fish to look for the key.

Off swam the fish, but though they searched and searched for it they could not find the key and came back without it.

"It isn't there!" said they.

At this Teeny-Tiny flung the sword that smote of itself into the sea again, and the sword began cutting off the heads of the big fishes.

"Tell your sword to spare my kin, you shall have your key!" the Whale-Fish cried.

He summoned crabs and lobsters and other such creatures and ordered them to look for the key. But though they searched and searched for it they could not find the key and came up without it.

The Whale-Fish looked at them and saw that all of them were there save for one lobster; he looked again, and there was the lobster crawling up to him!

"Here is the key!" said he. "It was stuck deep in the sand."

The Whale-Fish turned to Teeny-Tiny.

"Get on your horse!" he cried. "I will throw you the key when I know you to be three hundred miles away from here."

Away rode Teeny-Tiny, and when he had left three hundred miles behind him he heard the key swish through the air as it flew toward him. He stretched out his arms and caught it, and lo!—there he was back in the tsar's palace again.

The tsar was overjoyed. He promoted Teeny-Tiny to colonel and then asked Volinka to marry him and not to put the wedding off any longer.

"I will not be married in that old church of yours!" Volinka said. "Have another, made of gold and silver and with a gold and silver bridge leading to it built on the river's opposite bank. A vineyard must be planted around it, and you must see to it that it is in bloom when we are on our way to church and the grapes ready to be picked when we are on our way back. In front of the church a ditch twelve metres deep and twelve wide must be dug, a fire made up in the ditch, and a cauldron filled with tar hung over the fire. And inside the church candles must be lit and a choir must sing. And mind,

I will only marry you if all this is done in the space of one night!"

It could not be helped, so the tsar sent for Teeny-Tiny again and ordered him to do as Volinka bade.

"I will never be able to do it, Your Majesty!" Teeny-Tiny said.

"Don't refuse or your head you'll lose!" the tsar cried.

Teeny-Tiny hung his head.

"Give me two days to think how I am to go about it, Your Majesty," he said, and the tears pouring from his eyes, off he went to see his horse.

"Why do you weep, Teeny-Tiny?" the horse asked.

"How can I help it when I am soon to die!"

"To die?"

"Yes. For never can I do what the tsar wants me to do."

"And what is that?"

"I am to build a church of gold and silver on the river's opposite bank, to plant a vineyard round it and to dig a ditch twelve metres deep and twelve wide in front of it. In the church candles must be lit and a choir must sing, and a cauldron filled with tar must be hung over a fire made up in the ditch. And all this is to be done in the space of one night."

"Now, that is not an easy task, I must say, and I cannot help you with it," the horse said. "I can only give you this

94

counsel: go to see Volinka and beg her to come to your aid. Who knows!—she may well take pity on you."

It could not be helped, so Teeny-Tiny went to see Volinka, and bowing low to her, begged her to help him.

Volinka felt sorry for Teeny-Tiny.

"Don't you grieve, Teeny-Tiny," said she. "Say your prayers and go to bed, and everything will be done for you. And when morning comes make yourself a broom, sweep the bridge and then go and tell the tsar that everything is ready."

Teeny-Tiny thanked Volinka, went to his chamber, said his prayers and got into bed. But he kept thinking of what was in store for him and could not sleep.

Morning came, he went to the river bank, and lo!—everything had been done. The church was there, and the bridge, and the vineyard, and the ditch.

So he went to see the tsar and told him about it.

"I did as you bade me do, Your Majesty," he said. "The church has been built, and you can get married in it."

The tsar was overjoyed and had Teeny-Tiny made prince.

And Teeny-Tiny took a broom and spent the morning sweeping and cleaning the bridge.

As for Volinka and the tsar, they put on their finery and set out for the church from whose open doors came the sound of the choir singing. Around the church the grapevines were in bloom and in front of it a fire was burning with a tar-filled cauldron hanging over it.

They came up to the ditch, and Volinka told the tsar to cross it.

"I will go after you," said she. "The goose always follows the gander."

The tsar did not do as she said. Instead, he called Teeny-Tiny and ordered him to cross the ditch. This Teeny-Tiny did, but the tsar, who went after him, fell into the cauldron and was boiled to death!

As for Volinka, she crossed the ditch, took Teeny-Tiny by the hand and led him into the church. They were married then and there and went back to the palace together.

And as they walked on they could only stare, for the grapes had all ripened and the vines were picked bare. Teeny-Tiny was happy and held a grand feast, one to startle the world at the very least, and the two lived together in good health and good cheer and prospered the more with each passing year. I attended the feast and I drank ale and wine, and it ran fast as fast can be down this beard of mine.

As I was leaving for home they gave me a horse made of tar for a present, a saddle made of burdock and a whip made of peas.

I started on my way, and there, just ahead, was a threshing floor in flames! I began trying to put out the fire, but my horse melted away, my saddle was eaten by pigs and my whip pecked by crows. *So then I began to trade in wood, but for all I tried I never made good.*

MOLDAVIAN FOLK TALES

How Ionike Fet-Frumos Freed the Sun
Retold by *Natalia Gesse* and *Zoya Zadunaiskaya*

The Pot of Gold
Retold by *Mikhail Bulatov*

Translated by *Irina Zheleznova*
Illustrations by *Isai Kirmu*

HOW IONIKE FET-FRUMOS FREED THE SUN

When it all happened my tale will not tell you, but I know it did long, long ago, for the sun never rose then nor gave of its warmth and light, a pall of darkness lay over all, and sorrow reigned on earth.

But the old people spoke of an even earlier time when night had been followed by day which brought with it blue skies and bright sunshine. They said that it was only later that the dragons had come and stolen the sun, hiding it none knew where.

Now, it was in the time of darkness that there lived on the edge of the forest a man and his wife. The man worked very, very hard, but the couple were very poor, and there were days when there was nothing to eat in the house, not even a crust of bread.

One day the man came home and said to his wife:

"The people of this land, those who are as poor as you

and me, are going to try to find the sun and free it. I am joining them."

And though his wife wept and cried she could not stop him. He went away and never came back, and it was as if the earth had swallowed him.

The woman was left all alone, but soon a son was born to her, and she took joy in the sight of him and was happy.

The boy was given the name of Ion, but she always called him Ionike Fet-Frumos, Fet-Frumos being Moldavian for my lovely little son.

Ionike was a boy like no other. He was not yet three when he began helping his mother with her chores in the house and in the fields. But though they both worked very hard they were as poor as ever.

One day Ionike asked his mother to tell him about his father.

"Maybe I can do what my father did and follow in his footsteps," said he.

The mother, who feared for her son, burst into tears, but Ionike kept asking about his father again and again, and there came a day when she could not keep the truth from him any longer.

Ionike was deeply moved by what his mother told him. Never again after that could he forget that there had once been a time when the sun gave the earth of its light and warmth. He would think of the sun as he worked, he would see it in his dreams, and he even made a song about it which he would sing wherever it was he went and whatever it was he was doing.

This was the song:

> *"It was the dragons that stole the bright sun*
> *And carried it far away.*
> *One who is brave, one who is strong*
> *Will come and free it some day.*
> *Then will the earth know gladness anew,*
> *For sunshine will banish night;*
> *Then will the fields be golden with wheat,*
> *Pleasing the heart and sight.*
> *When I grow up, when in wisdom I gain,*
> *When myself to be strong I know,*
> *A sword I will take and a cudgel as well*
> *And in search of the bright sun go."*

One day Ionike was in the forest gathering brushwood and singing his song when the ruler of the realm who went by the name of the Black Tsar because he was blind happened to be driving by there in his coach.

"I have everything my heart desires, everything save the sun," said he to himself when he heard the song. "Now, if only I could get the sun for myself too, I would have the whole of the earth in my power."

He ordered his servants to stop the horses and to fetch the singer.

The servants seized Ionike Fet-Frumos and brought him to the tsar who asked him if it was he who had been singing about the sun.

"Yes indeed," said Ionike. "I made up the song myself. I sang about something I mean to do."

The tsar knew by Ionike's voice that he was very young.

"What is your name, lad?" he asked.

"Ionike. But they call me Ionike Fet-Frumos," Ionike told him.

"Listen to me, Ionike," the tsar said. "If you really want to free the sun, then I will be only too glad to help you. You will live with me in my palace where you will have all you need to make you very strong. And when the time comes for you to set out on your journey you shall have a good sword and a fine horse. Now, are you coming with me?"

"I would if only I did not have to leave my mother all alone," Ionike said.

"That needn't stop us!" said the tsar. "She can live in the palace too."

After that there was nothing more Ionike could say, and the tsar took him with him to his palace. But when the tsar's servants came for Ionike's mother, she refused to go with them and asked them to give Ionike her love and to tell him that she would await his return in their house.

Ionike Fet-Frumos lived in the palace for a number of years, and with every day that passed he grew stronger and stronger. He had only to strike a rock with the side of his hand for it to split in two, and he had only to squeeze a stone for it to break up into tiny pieces.

At last came the day when Ionike decided that it was time to set out on his journey, and when he heard about it the tsar sent for him and told him to choose a sword and a cudgel for himself and a horse as well.

Ionike chose a sword that was the sharpest and a cudgel that was the heaviest of any that were offered him and then went to the stable. The horses there were all handsome and sleek, but he had only to touch one for it to fall to the ground.

This made Ionike very angry.

"I don't want any of these horses!" he said.

He looked round him and saw a colt he had not noticed before in the far corner of the stable. The colt was small and skinny and his mane was dirty and matted, and as he came up to him he stamped his hooves and whinnied.

"A pitiful little thing, never would I take it for myself!" said Ionike, slapping the colt's back.

But unlike the other horses the colt did not fall and only stretched out his neck to him as if asking him to bridle him and promising to serve him faithfully.

Ionike bridled him, and lo!—the colt shook himself and turned into a handsome stallion, one whose like could not be found anywhere! Ionike saddled him and jumped on his back, and he at once set off at a trot, the sparks flying from under his hooves and lighting the way as he ran and the earth quaking and rumbling beneath him and starting an echo in the mountains.

Whether Ionike was on his way for a short or a long time nobody knows, but he and his horse were tired, so, seeing a bridge spanning a river before him, he stopped the horse, set him free to graze on the bank and himself lay down there for a sleep.

He closed his eyes and was dozing away when he heard the pounding of a horse's hooves on the river's opposite bank. The sound grew louder as the horse galloped up to the bridge, and Ionike opened his eyes just in time to see it start and back away with a snort. The man mounted on the horse struck it with his whip.

"You old nag you, may the wolves eat you up, what are you scared of? You boasted that you feared none save that great hero, Ionike Fet-Frumos!" he cried.

Ionike sprang to his feet.

"I am Ionike Fet-Frumos! No wonder your horse is frightened," said he loudly.

At this the man let out a bellow of laughter, and so loud was it that the river was furrowed by waves.

"Brave, aren't you!" he cried. "Don't you know me? I am Dusk, the dragon who carried away the sun and locked it in a dungeon. Be off with you!"

"I'll not go away, let us fight, Dusk!" Ionike returned.

Dusk jumped from his horse's back and came at Ionike. He lifted him high and then threw him down so that Ionike was driven up to his ankles into the ground. But Ionike fought back and had soon driven the dragon into the ground up to his knees. Both of them were flushed now and breathing hard, and Dusk grabbed Ionike, and raising him high over his head, swung him round and round and then drove him into the ground up to his waist. But this only angered Ionike the more. He gathered all of his strength and flung the dragon over his shoulder, driving him into the ground up to his neck. Then, pulling his sword from its scabbard, he smote off the

dragon's head. After that he mounted his horse and rode away.

On and on he rode till he came to another bridge spanning another river. He stopped his horse, and saying to himself "I think I'll take a rest, for who knows what is in store for me!" set him free to graze on the bank. Then, sitting down by the side of the road, he began singing his song.

"It was the dragons that stole the bright sun
And carried it far away.
One who is brave, one who is strong
Will come and free it some day!" he sang.

And he had only just sung the last line when he heard the clatter of a horse's hooves—clip-clop!—coming from the river's opposite bank. The horse galloped up to the bridge, but instead of crossing it, started and backed away with a snort.

"A bait for the wolves and a treat for the ravens, that's what you are, you old nag you!" the rider cried. "Why do you back away? You told me that none could frighten you save Ionike Fet-Frumos!"

"I am Ionike Fet-Frumos!" Ionike Fet-Frumos cried. "And who may you be?"

"I am Evening, the brother of Dusk, and you are as nothing

compared to me!" the dragon told him. "I have only to blow once, and every living thing on earth will drop dead. So let us fight if you won't make way for me!"

They began to fight, they fought long and hard, and in the end it was Ionike Fet-Frumos who vanquished Evening. He drove him up to his neck into the ground and then he smote off his head.

After that he had a drink of water, watered his horse and rode on.

Over hills and dales he rode and over fields and forests and he only stopped when he came to a third bridge spanning a third river. And no sooner had he jumped to the ground than he saw a horse and a rider galloping up to the bridge on the river's opposite bank. But the horse stopped short when it reached the bridge and would go no further.

Seeing it, Ionike's own horse turned his head and looked at him.

"The two battles you fought are as nothing compared to the one you now face," said he in low tones, "for Midnight the Dragon himself is there before you. But fear nothing, for you will vanquish him!"

Ionike and Midnight began to fight, and never had there been a fiercer battle. Midnight came at Ionike and with his first blow drove him up to his chest into the ground. But

this did not stop Ionike who seized the dragon and drove him into the ground up to his neck. He pulled out his sword and was about to smite off the dragon's head, but the dragon scrambled out of the pit and came at him again! They fought for a long time, but neither could overcome the other, and so weak were they now that they dropped to the ground, both of them, and lay there, hardly being able to take breath.

All of a sudden what should they hear but the whirring of wings coming from overhead! They looked up, and there, wheeling just above them, was a kite!

"Please, kite, sprinkle some water over me and give me back my strength!" Midnight cried. "I will kill Ionike Fet-Frumos, and you will eat your fill of his flesh."

"Please, kite, my brother, sprinkle some water over me and give me back my strength!" Ionike cried. "I will free the sun, and you will bask in its rays and warm yourself!"

The kite made no reply. He dropped down on to the river, and scooping up some water with his wing, sprinkled Ionike with it. Then he dropped down a second time, and drawing some water into his beak, gave it to Ionike to drink.

Ionike was filled with fresh strength. Up he jumped, and falling on the dragon, cut him in two with his sword.

"Thank you for helping me, kite!" he cried. "And now

tell me where I am to find the sun. You fly everywhere and must know where it is!"

"Ride straight on and don't stop till you reach the forest," the kite said. "The dragons' castle is just beyond it, and I think you will find the sun in one of the castle dungeons. But you are much too trustful. Strength is no match for cunning."

"I have enough cunning for both of us!" said Ionike's horse.

"Well, then, be off with you, and may good luck attend you!" the kite cried.

Ionike rode on, and whether a short or a long time passed nobody knows, but he came to a forest, and so dense was it that he could neither ride through it nor pass through it on foot.

Ionike's horse stopped.

"Only a fly can hope to pass through this forest," he said. "Pluck a hair from my mane and tie it round your waist, and you will turn into one. After that fly to the castle and try to find out where the sun is kept, the dragons will be sure to talk about it. And if you want to get back your proper shape, just light on the ground. I will wait for you here."

Ionike did as the horse said, and turning into a fly, made his way to the castle. He flew all around it, trying to find an

opening or a crack in the wall through which to fly inside. In the end he got into the castle through the chimney flue, and lo!—sitting at a table there and talking were the mother of Dusk, Evening and Midnight and their three wives.

Ionike remembered his horse's warning and kept very quiet.

"Where can my sons be, I'm worried about them," said the dragons' mother. "I could always hear the clatter of their horses' hooves before, but now there's not a sound. Could they have met with some misfortune?"

"Nonsense, Mother, whom have they to fear!" said her daughter-in-law.

"Ionike Fet-Frumos, that's whom! He was destined from birth to free the sun."

"A curse on this Ionike Fet-Frumos!" said Dusk's wife. "Even if he should succeed in freeing the sun, he will not feast his eyes on it long. When he sets out on his journey home, I will turn into a well, and he will drink some of my water and die."

"And I will turn into an apple-tree," said Evening's wife. "He will take a bite of an apple of mine and drop dead."

"Good!" said Midnight's wife. "As for me, I will turn into a grapevine. He will eat a grape of mine and drop dead."

"You mustn't boast, my dears, for it will lead to nothing good," said the dragons' mother. "Better go and see if the sun is safely in the dungeon still."

The dragons' wives went down into the dungeon, and Ionike flew after them.

Standing in the dungeon was a chest bound with iron, and when they saw a sun ray stealing through a chink in it, the dragons' wives did not even lift the lid.

"It's just as we thought, the sun is in the chest!" said they. "Our mother-in-law is always imagining things!" And with that they left the dungeon.

No sooner were they gone than Ionike got back his proper shape and lifted the chest lid, and the sun floated out of the chest, burnt its way through the dungeon's oaken doors and soared up to the sky. It lit up the earth with its rays, and lo!—the birds began to sing, and the people to smile and embrace one another. Never before had there been such rejoicing!

The Black Tsar alone did not rejoice. He had wanted the sun to be his alone, and that was why he had had Ionike live in his palace. Dark with fury, he climbed up on to the palace roof, and wanting to seize the sun, reached for it with both hands.

But he misstepped and fell to the ground, and that was the

end of him. And if you think that anyone grieved for him, you are mistaken.

As for Ionike Fet-Frumos, he followed the sun out of the dungeon, got on his horse and set out on his journey home.

The sun shone overhead, and not being used to this, he felt hot and uncomfortable despite his joy. And oh! how thirsty he was, so thirsty that he could hardly bear it! He looked about him and saw a well by the wayside. The water in it was as clear as crystal, and he was about to take a drink when he remembered what Dusk's wife had said. So he struck the side of the well with his sword, and when a stream of black blood ran out of it, he knew that Dusk's wife was dead.

Ionike rode on, and he was as thirsty as ever. He looked about him, and he saw an apple-tree growing by the wayside, the apples on it rosy and fresh and fairly asking to be eaten. Ionike struck the apple-tree with his sword, and there, on the road before him, lay Evening's wife, dead.

Ionike rode on again, looking about him for a sight of the grapevine with the poisoned grapes. He saw it soon enough and struck it with his sword, and now Midnight's wife was dead too.

Of the dragons' whole family their mother alone was still alive, and what she might have turned herself into Ionike could not guess. He looked up at the sky, and he saw a black

cloud cut by zigzags of lightning moving swiftly across it. The thunder crashed, and Ionike knew that the cloud was the dragons' mother. She was almost upon him now, and as she opened wide her jaws, the upper part touching the sky and the lower, the earth, flame poured out of them.

Ionike spurred on his horse, and the horse turned off the road and carried him into a smithy which stood by the wayside. Ionike shut and bolted the door, and he was just in time, for the dragons' mother was very close. She tried to smash the roof and to break down the door, but not being able to do it, decided to use cunning.

"Please, Ionike Fet-Frumos, let me take a look at you, for never have I seen anyone so brave!" said she in the sweetest of voices.

"Why not! Just wait a moment!" Ionike told her.

He fanned the flames in the forge, held his cudgel with its steel pins over it till it was red-hot and then made a hole in the wall. The dragons' mother put her head through it, Ionike sprang aside and held out the red-hot cudgel, and she swallowed it and dropped dead.

There was nothing more to fear, so Ionike opened wide the smithy door, and lo!—the black cloud was gone, and the sun shone overhead.

Ionike got on his horse and rode on till he reached

his own realm where he was welcomed by all. He came to his village and stopped his horse in front of his hut, and his mother ran out, weeping, and threw her arms about him. And those were her last tears, for she knew only joy and happiness and never had cause to weep any more.

THE POT OF GOLD

Once upon a time there lived a man who had three sons. He was a hardworking man and laboured from morn till night. But his sons did not take after their father. They were strong and healthy lads, all three, but terrible loafers who did not want to do anything at all.

The father worked in the field, in the garden and in the house, but his sons sat chatting in the shade under the trees or went to the Dniester for a day's fishing.

"Why do you never help your father?" their neighbours asked.

"Why should we!" the sons replied. "Father takes good care of us and does all the work very well by himself."

And so it went from year to year.

The sons grew to manhood, and the father aged and could no longer work as before. The garden round the house ran wild and the field was overgrown with weeds. The sons saw this, but were so lazy that they would do nothing about it.

"Why do you sit there, my sons, idling the hours away?" their father would ask them. "I worked hard all my life, and now your turn has come to do the same."

But no matter what he said, his sons would not listen to him and did nothing but twiddle their thumbs.

So troubled was the old man that his sons were such loafers that he fell ill and took to his bed.

By now the family were in the direst need. Nettles and thistles grew so thick around the hut that it was barely visible.

One day the old man called his sons to his bedside.

"My end has come, my sons," said he. "How are you going to live without me, loafers that you are?"

The sons burst into tears.

"Give us your last counsel, Father," the eldest son begged. "Tell us what we are to do."

"Very well!" said the father. "I'll tell you a secret. You know that your mother and I toiled hard and ceaselessly. Over the years, bit by bit, we were able to put aside what we earned till we had a potful of gold. I buried the pot near the house, only I don't remember just where. Find it, and you will be rich and never know need."

With that he bade his sons goodbye and breathed his last.

The sons were deeply grieved and they wept and sorrowed for a long time. One day the eldest of them said:

"Well, brothers, we are poor indeed, we haven't even money enough to buy bread with. Let us do as our father bade before he died and look for the pot of gold."

They took their spades and began digging near the hut, they dug and they dug, but they could not find the pot of gold.

Said the middle brother:

"If we dig like this, my brothers, we will never find the pot. Let us dig up the ground all around the hut!"

The brothers agreed. They took up their spades again and they dug up the ground all around the hut, but no pot of gold did they find.

"Let us dig some more, but deeper," said the youngest brother. "Perhaps father buried the pot of gold deep down."

Once again the brothers agreed: they were very eager to find the pot.

They set to work, and the eldest brother, who had been digging a long time, suddenly felt his spade strike something quite big and hard. His heart pounding wildly, for he thought that he had found the pot of gold, he called to his brothers, to come to him quickly.

The two brothers came running and began helping their elder brother dig.

They worked very, very hard, but what they dug up from the ground was not a pot of gold, but a large stone.

The brothers were disappointed.

"What shall we do with the stone?" said they. "It's no use leaving it here. Let us carry it away and throw it in a gully."

No sooner said than done. They got rid of the stone and began digging again. They worked all day long, never stopping to eat or rest, and they dug up the whole of the garden. The soil under their spades became nice and soft, but for all their efforts no pot of gold did they find.

"Now that we have dug up the garden, it's no use leaving things as they are, let us plant grapevines here!" said the eldest brother.

"That's a good idea!" the two younger brothers agreed. "At least our labours will not have been wasted."

So they planted some grapevines and began tending them carefully.

A short time passed, and they had a fine, large vineyard where ripened good, juicy grapes.

The brothers gathered a rich harvest. They put aside the grapes they needed for themselves and sold the rest at a profit.

Said the eldest brother:

"It was not in vain, after all, that we dug up our garden for we found the treasure of which father spoke before he died."

Lyudmila Loboda and Ivan Ostafiichuk illustrated the two Ukrainian tales in this book, "The Poor Man and the Tsar of the Crows" and "The Flying Ship".

Both artists won diplomas at exhibitions of book illustrations at home and abroad. Some of Lyudmila Loboda's and Ivan Ostafiichuk's drawings are in the possession of the Tretyakov Gallery, the State Museum of Art of the Ukrainian Republic and in the art museums of Lvov, Voronezh and Dnepropetrovsk.

The young Byelorussian artist Vladimir Savich is a graduate of the Academy of Arts of the USSR. His works were exhibited many times both at home and abroad and won him a number of prizes and diplomas.

Vladimir Savich illustrated the one Byelorussian tale in this book, "Teeny-Tiny".

*English translation © Raduga Publishers 1986

Winner of sixty diplomas of All-Union and Republican competitions of book illustrations, Isai Kirmu designed and illustrated over two hundred books, and took part in a number of international exhibitions.

Isai Kirmu illustrated the two Moldavian tales in this book, "How Ionike Fet-Frumos Freed the Sun" and "The Pot of Gold".

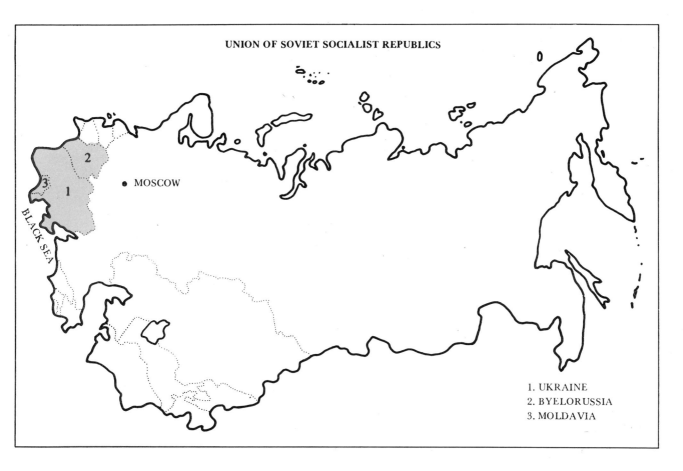

UNION OF SOVIET SOCIALIST REPUBLICS

MOSCOW

BLACK SEA

1. UKRAINE
2. BYELORUSSIA
3. MOLDAVIA

The peoples of the Ukraine, Byelorussia and Moldavia are known for their industry, hospitality and their love for their native land. Their traditional ties with the Russian people were greatly strengthened after the Great October Socialist Revolution of 1917 when the three backward provinces of tsarist Russia became socialist republics. In the years that have passed since, each of these republics has attained an economic and cultural progress that could never have been dreamt of before.

There is much that the Ukrainian, Byelorussian and Moldavian peoples have in common. This is manifested in their love of art, their colourful songs and spirited dances, the brightness of their national costumes, their ways and habits.

The folk tales of the three peoples bear signs of having had identical sources with those of the Russian folk tales. There are any number of migrant themes that have found their way into them and that lead to a similarity of subject matter. At the same time their national characteristics remain preserved. Baba-Yaga the Witch and Zmei Gorinich, the Dragon of the Russian tales, have their counterparts in Ukrainian, Byelorussian and Moldavian tales. It is not always easy to determine the origins of that or the other tale so old and so strong are the cultural ties linking the three or, rather, the four peoples.

The tales in this book, each having its own national flavour, will introduce readers to the rich folklore of the three republics.

REQUEST TO READERS

Raduga Publishers would be glad to have your opinion of this book, its translation and design and any suggestions you may have for future publications.

Please send all your comments to 17, Zubovsky Boulevard, Moscow, USSR.

Сказки народов Украины, Белоруссии и Молдавии

СКАЗКИ НАРОДОВ СССР

На английском языке

© Состав, иллюстрации, аппарат. Издательство ''Радуга'', 1986 г.

Printed in the Union of Soviet Socialist Republics